STEWART FALLS

W9-AJR-428

TAGALONG ALLIE'S
BURROW

When I Grow Up

To my daughter Allie, my little princess, who I never want to grow up
—Sean Covey

For Charles Schulz, who gave me an end in mind
—Stacy Curtis

SIMON & SCHUSTER BOOKS FOR YOUNG READERS
An imprint of Simon & Schuster Children's Publishing Division
1230 Avenue of the Americas, New York, New York 10020
Copyright © 2009 by Franklin Covey Co.
All rights reserved, including the right of reproduction in whole or in part in any form.
SIMON & SCHUSTER BOOKS FOR YOUNG READERS is a trademark of Simon & Schuster, Inc.

Book design by Laurent Linn
The text for this book is set in Montara Gothic.
The illustrations for this book are rendered in pencil and watercolor.
Manufactured in the United States of America
2 4 6 8 10 9 7 5 3 1

CIP data for this book is available from the Library of Congress.
ISBN: 978-1-4169-9424-4
Guaranteed Reinforced Binding   0909

When I Grow Up

SEAN COVEY

Illustrated by Stacy Curtis

SIMON & SCHUSTER BOOKS FOR YOUNG READERS

New York   London   Toronto   Sydney

It was time for Tagalong Allie to go to bed.

Allie snuggled under her covers

as Granny read her a story about a little girl who grew up.

Granny finished the story and gave Allie a kiss.

"Time to go to sleep," said Granny.

After Granny left, Allie lay wide awake.

"When I get bigger," said Allie, "I wanna gwow up too."

She imagined what it would be like to be all grown up.

She could wear lots of makeup

and jewelry,

walk to the grocery store all by herself,

make yummy food,

write her very own book,

go to work,

hike to Stewart Falls,

and even fly to the moon.

"But first," said Allie, "I need to . . .

go to school,

do my chores,

say my pwayers,

and go to sleep.

Then I can gwow up."

Allie turned over,

closed her eyes,

and fell sound asleep.

PARENTS' CORNER

HABIT ② —Begin with the End in Mind: *Have a Plan*

I REMEMBER TUCKING MY OWN **A**LLIE INTO BED ONE NIGHT WHILE SHE TOLD ME ABOUT all the things she wanted to do when she grew up, like having a baby, driving a car, and making yummy food, hopefully not in that order. I was impressed with how well she could picture the future at the mere age of three. "All kids are born geniuses. However, by the time they turn eight, 99 percent of them are de-genius-ized by grown-ups," or so said Albert Schweitzer. Truly, children are blessed with the gift of imagination, which is one of the four gifts that make us human, along with conscience, self-awareness, and willpower. And we should do all we can to nurture imagination, not smother it. After all, this is what beginning with the end in mind is all about. It's about visualizing the end state you want, whether it be in a job, a relationship, or a feeling, and then working to achieve it. All things are created twice, you see. First in the mind's eye . . . then for real. Just ask Helen Keller, Mahatma Gandhi, Superman, or Cinderella.

In this story, highlight how Allie begins with the end in mind. She imagines how much fun it will be to grow up and shop, cook, hike, and even fly. She creates this future in her mind's eye in vivid detail. But she then realizes that to get what she wants tomorrow, she must do the little things today, like doing her chores, brushing her teeth, and going to bed.

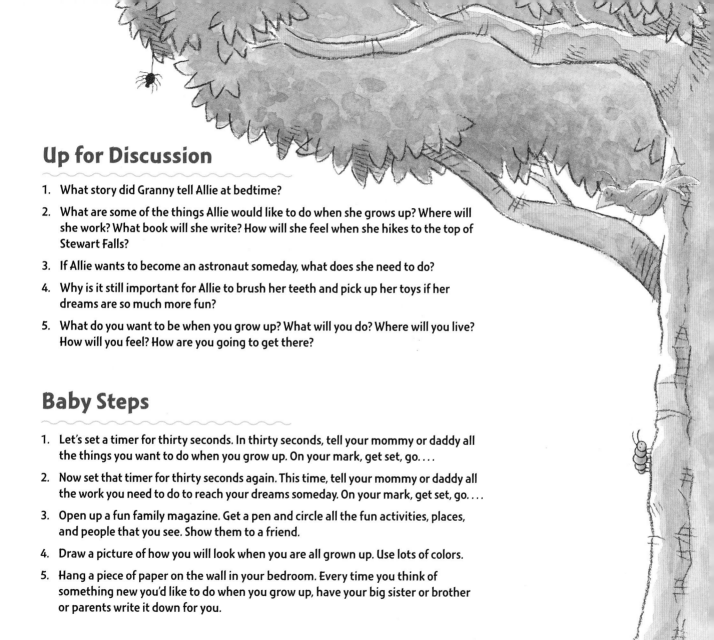

Up for Discussion

1. What story did Granny tell Allie at bedtime?

2. What are some of the things Allie would like to do when she grows up? Where will she work? What book will she write? How will she feel when she hikes to the top of Stewart Falls?

3. If Allie wants to become an astronaut someday, what does she need to do?

4. Why is it still important for Allie to brush her teeth and pick up her toys if her dreams are so much more fun?

5. What do you want to be when you grow up? What will you do? Where will you live? How will you feel? How are you going to get there?

Baby Steps

1. Let's set a timer for thirty seconds. In thirty seconds, tell your mommy or daddy all the things you want to do when you grow up. On your mark, get set, go. . . .

2. Now set that timer for thirty seconds again. This time, tell your mommy or daddy all the work you need to do to reach your dreams someday. On your mark, get set, go. . . .

3. Open up a fun family magazine. Get a pen and circle all the fun activities, places, and people that you see. Show them to a friend.

4. Draw a picture of how you will look when you are all grown up. Use lots of colors.

5. Hang a piece of paper on the wall in your bedroom. Every time you think of something new you'd like to do when you grow up, have your big sister or brother or parents write it down for you.